Contents

The jewels of Geranius   2
Terry Deary

The world next door   23
Joan Aiken

The bus stop that ate children   39
Susan Gates

The greatest drummer in the world   48
Leon Rosselson

The jewels of Geranius

These are the messages from Starship Space Eagle – a two-person spaceship. Its mission was to explore the stars, make alien friends… and generally stay out of trouble.

It was the first British spaceship ever built.

Of course it all went wrong!

With Captain Dan Darenot in charge it was bound to.

Dan went to Space College. He took all the exams – and failed them.

Golden Moon Space College

Student Report   Student: Daniel Darenot

Subject	Mark	Comment	Pass
Astronomy	3/100	Thinks Mars is a bar of chocolate and the moon's a ball of green cheese. He couldn't find Pluto if he was sitting on it. Hopeless!	Fail
Starship Driving	2/100	Darenot shouldn't be allowed to drive a pair of roller skates. He's more clumsy than a chimp with a chain-saw in a china shop. Dreadful!	Fail
Computers	1/100	This man has the brain of a cunning fox – but the fox wants it back. Can't even work a pocket calculator. Useless!	Fail
Self Defence	0/100	Known as Dangerous Dan – in the last three years he has caused five broken noses, four broken arms and three broken legs – luckily they were all his own! A disaster!	Fail
Personal	100/100	This man doesn't know the meaning of fear. (And he can't spell it either.) He's strong as a butterfly and has the brains of a brick. But he's cheerful, kind and tries hard. A really nice man.	Pass

They didn't send him into space because he was the *best* space captain. They sent him because he was the *worst!* It didn't matter if he didn't come back!

Dan was given just one chance. They gave him a helper to pilot the Starship Space Eagle – they gave him Space Cadet Betty Yett.

Betty was the best pupil at space-school… they wanted rid of her too. She was too clever. Always telling her teachers what was right.

And she talked too much. "Bossy Betty", they called her.

Would they find a pathway to the stars?

Would they come back rich and famous?

Would Space Eagle get off the ground?

These are the messages that give the answers. They

tell the greatest adventure since Red Riding Hood ate the Three Little Pigs, the most fantastic voyage since Goldilocks went to Wonderland... and the greatest romance since Cinderella stuck the glass slipper on Prince Charming's left ear.

MESSAGE ONE

TIME: 14.30 hours
DATE: 1 April 2190

This is Space Eagle to Base... Space Eagle to Base... are you receiving me? Are you receiving me?

Are you deaf?

Oh, never mind. I'll send the message anyway. I hope you can reply later.

This is Captain Dan Darenot of Space Eagle calling. I have landed with my pilot, Space Cadet Betty Yett, on the planet Geranius.

This is a great shame, because we were aiming for the planet Mars. I told her we should have turned left at the moon. But did she listen to me? No, she never does!

Ah, well, we'll just have to make the most of it. I am setting off now to boldly explore the turquoise trees, the purple plants and petrifying people of the planet Geranius.

This is Captain Darenot boldly signing off.

CAPTAIN'S LOG: STAR DATE 1-4-2190

Landed on the planet Geranius. Captain has left Space Eagle to explore planet. No signs of life… yet. Space Cadet Betty Yett left in charge of Space Eagle.

Captain Darenot is a fat fool – he did tell me to turn left at the moon. The trouble is he meant to tell me to turn right! He can't tell the difference. He's gone off exploring now with his space boots on the wrong feet!

What a clown! If he didn't have me to look after him he'd have tried to land on the Sun!

I'm bored. I've played all the computer games on the ship. I win every time. Maybe I'll try drawing.

Geranius Planet

Captain Darenot

Betty

MESSAGE TWO

TIME: 16.30 hours
DATE: 1 April 2190

This is Space Eagle to Base... Space Eagle to Base. Are you receiving me? Please let me know if you're not!

We have a problem already.

I have met a native of Geranius ... a Geranium ... and she isn't pleased to see me. Probably because Cadet Yett landed in the middle of her flower-bed.

She spoke to me in Geranian.

She said, "Gerroff-me-planet-before-I-kick-you-off-you-fat-alien!" The computer translated this into English. It means "Gerroff me planet before I kick you off you fat alien!"

Being bold and brave I didn't let her bully me. Just because she's three metres tall with a three-eyed, green face like a mouldy boot. I looked her straight in the knee-cap and told her. I did! I told her straight. I said, "Sorry, madam!"

She replied, "Push off or else!"

I decided it was a good time to push off.

I can't explore the planet because this Geranium woman will kick me with one of her twenty-kilo clogs – maybe with all three of her clogs!

I need a disguise. I need to look like a strange inhuman Geranium alien. Cadet Yett has made me a costume based on a Geranium man she saw. I am boldly going out in this disguise now.

This is Captain Darenot signing off.

First contact made with alien natives of Geranius. Captain Darenot tried to make contact but the alien female did not want to talk. Captain will return dressed as a Geranium and try again.

Darenot is a fat fool and cowardly captain. But he should be fine in the brilliant alien costume I made for him.

I got the idea from a picture on Geranium TV. I think it was a pop music show. This Geranium was singing, "Give me a kiss with your slimy green lips." The

singer had two arms like tentacles but only one hand – perhaps he needs to go to a second-hand shop! He has green teeth and orange hair with three yellow Geranium eyes and a cute dimple in each of his chins. The Captain put the costume on – he looks quite handsome now! Only joking, of course.

I wish old Darenot would hurry back. I'm hungry and I want my tea. The Captain may be a fat fool and a rotten starship driver, but he cooks beautiful moon-beans on toast. And I want to know how my costume idea worked.

MESSAGE THREE

TIME: 18.30 hours
DATE: 1 April 2190

This is Space Eagle to Base! Space Eagle to Base! This is Space Beagle to Ace! Are you receiving me? Are you receiving me?

Are you asleep?

I suppose you must be. Cadet Yett has really dropped me in it this time... and I don't mean in a Geranium flower patch! I mean in real trouble.

Bossy Betty flew me down in her space taxi.

"Good luck, Captain," she smiled. She's quite pretty when she smiles. "I'll worry about you."

"I don't need to be lucky," I told her. "I need to be skilful, clever and fearless."

"I know," she sighed. "That's why I'll worry about you!"

As she flew back to the starship I boldly strode out in my Geranium costume ... and it's not easy boldly striding anywhere when you have three legs!

Suddenly I heard a scream like a wounded frog!

It was the three-eyed Geranium woman with the face like a melted wellie.

"Dason!" she screeched.

"Me? Dason?" I asked as she rushed towards me.

"Dason-Jonovan!"

"Me? Dason-Jonovan?" I gulped.

"Dason-Jonovan pop star!" she said as she stretched her tentacles towards me.

She thought I was some Geranium pop star called Dason
Jonovan! Betty's costume was too good!

"Me-Krawlie!" the Geranium gurgled and wrapped her
tentacle round my neck. It was cold and slimy. Yeuch! "Me
Krawlie!" she kept saying.

"Your name is Krawlie?" I could guess why ... she made my
flesh crawl!

"Krawlie-Me-Lug."

"Nice name," I smiled.

"Saw you on telly," she grunted.

"Er..." I tried to back away – she just wrapped the tentacle
tighter.

"Love you Dason!" she squealed. "Marry me!"

"Errrk! Marry you?" I shuddered. What could I say? I said, "No!"

"Marry me or else!" she hissed.

Suddenly I had an idea. "I've got to go, Krawlie. I'm doing a concert in ten minutes. Tell you what... I'll come back after the concert and we'll talk about it then... OK?"

"Marry-Krawlie?" she gurgled.

"We'll... we'll talk about it," I promised. She loosened the tentacle.

I ran!

When I reached the shelter of a tree I called for Betty to pick me up in the space taxi.

Of course a space captain always keeps his word – I'll have to go back and see the hideous Krawlie... but not until I've had my tea.

This is Captain Dan Darenot signing off.

Captain Darenot has made contact with aliens again. After a food break he will return to talk to Miss Me-Lug.

Captain Darenot is a bit of a fibber. I'll tell you the truth ... but don't let on that I've told you! The real reason that he's going back to see Krawlie is not to keep his word. It's because when he ran away from Krawlie he dropped the starship starter key.

We can't escape from Geranius until he finds it. We're trapped on this perfectly putrid purple planet.

If he ends up married to the awful alien it will serve him right.

MESSAGE FOUR

TIME: 20.30 hours
DATE: 1 April 2190

This is Space Eagle to Base. Ace Peagle to mace! Are you receiving me? I'm not receiving you. I think I must be pressing the wrong buttons.

I've boldly been down to Geranius a second time. The creepsome Krawlie was waiting.

"Dason-Marry-Krawlie!" she burbled.

I took a deep breath and boldly said, "No!"

I waited for her to choke the life out of me with her slimy tentacle. But she didn't! Instead she waved the golden starship key in front of my nose. "Krawlie-got-Dason's-airplane key," she giggled and showed her pointed green teeth in an evil smile. "Dason-dropped-it!"

I asked her nicely. I begged and I pleaded but Krawlie wouldn't give me back the key. Not until I promised to marry her.

What could I do? I promised!

She's given me twenty-five Geranium hours to get her a diamond ring… or else, she says, she'll dunk my head in an enormous cup of geranium tea and eat me for supper. When she gets the ring then I get the key.

As you probably know there are plenty of diamonds on the planet Geranius. They're lying all over the ground. The trouble is I can't bend down to pick them up. My space-suit is too stiff. If I fall over I may never be able to get up again.

I asked Cadet Yett to design me a picker-upper that will pick up a jewel without me having to bend down and pick it up. She made a clever little arm with a claw on the end. In fact, Cadet Yett's a clever girl. I wonder if she'd help me make my model aeroplanes?

I'll have to hurry now. Twenty-five Geranium hours are just twenty-five Earth minutes.

This is Captain Darenot signing off.

P.S. Krawlie says you're all invited to the wedding.

CAPTAIN'S LOG: STAR DATE 1-4-2190

Captain Darenot has made friends with the alien. It seems the planet is covered with jewels. The captain will collect samples to bring back to Earth.

Captain Darenot is a fat fool and a cowardly Captain and uglier than ten Geranium Aliens... but I suppose I'll have to help him. I've made the picker-upper and sent Danny — that is, Captain Darenot — out to find a diamond.

Poor Dan will probably end up being eaten by the hideous Krawlie-Me-Lug. It'll serve him right — no, that's not true. He may be dimmer than a moonless night on Mars but he tries hard. I wouldn't like to see him married to an awful alien. He has a good heart. Pity he hasn't got a good brain to match.

I hope he'll be all right. And I hope he gets that key and looks after it.

MESSAGE FIVE

TIME: 22.30 hours
DATE: 1 April 2190

This is Space Eagle to Base. Space Biggle to Case. Base Giggle to Lace! This is Captain Darenot speaking from the planet Geranius.

So much for Cadet Yett's picker-upper design. I picker-upped a huge diamond and gave it to the hideous Krawlie-Me-Lug, the alien... and now the alien says I'm engaged to her.

Her only good point is the long black hair that flows all down her back – none on her head but stacks on her back.

I know my Space Captain Code. I know, I promised to boldly go where no human has boldly been before.

I didn't know that meant into Krawlie's loving arms!!

I can't stand her cuddles! They're not so much arms as tentacles with feathers on the end. They don't half tickle.

And she smells AWFUL!

Her perfume's called "Dead-cat-in-a-sweaty-sock".

I have the key for the Starship starter-motor. I also have an escape plan but I need Cadet Yett's help.

The trouble is Krawlie-Me-Lug is keeping a close eye on me. In fact she's keeping her three close eyes on me! I keep signalling to Cadet Yett in the starship on the hillside but she doesn't answer. Over and over again I signal:

"Fly Down in Space Eagle taxi. Pick me up at crossroads. Midnight. Captain Darenot."

This is Captain Darenot signing off.

P.S. Krawlie says she'd like an electric toaster as a wedding present.

CAPTAIN'S LOG: STAR DATE 1-4-2190

Message received from Captain on planet surface. Captain requests urgent rescue. Only Cadet Yett can reach him in time.

Poor Danny. I may save the tubby twit – if he agrees to do what I tell him. He may have the key to the starship starter-motor but I have the key to Space Eagle taxi, a little rocket that could fly down and rescue him. I won't let him in till he agrees to do what I want.

MESSAGE SIX

TIME: 00.30 hours
DATE: 2 April 2190

This is Space Eagle to Base. This is Space Eagle to Base. Are you receiving me? Have you all gone home and forgotten about me? I bet you have, you rotten lot.

That would be just the sort of rotten trick you would play on poor old Dan Darenot.

I remember back at Space College. You always used to call me names.

> "Dan, Dan, fat old man;
> Washed his face in a frying pan."

I remember. Well, I hope you're happy now. I am on my way home to Earth... and I'm very, very rich. My pockets are stuffed with the Jewels of Geranius.

But I will not be returning as Captain Dan Darenot.

Betty said I should give up this space captain job. She says I was never happy with it anyway.

You know, I think she's right! If I give up, I'll be home every night in time to play with my model aeroplanes.

Now it's ten seconds to lift-off and counting...

Nine	slippers in front of the fire
Eight	"Star Trek" on the telly
Seven	no more space-sickness
Six	I can have Pluto-burgers for tea

Five	no more food out of tubes
Four	I can sit in the garden
Three	no more moon dust up my nose
Two	friends round for dinner
One	and no more scary aliens!
ZERO	We have lift off!

See you in three weeks' time. This is Space Cadet Darenot signing off.

●●●●●●●●●●●●●●●●●●●●●●●●●●●●●●●●●●●●●●

CAPTAIN'S LOG: STAR DATE 2-4-2190

The Starship Space Eagle is now under the command of a new captain. Course set for Earth.

That's right. I rescued him… and I took over command of the ship. It wasn't easy, mind.

I flew Space Eagle taxi over to his hiding place and shouted through the window. I gave him his choice.

"Anything?" I asked.

"Anything… just open the door!"

"Say please."

"Open the door PLEASE!" he sobbed.

"Promise you'll let me be the captain of the Space Eagle!" I shouted.

"No! No! No! Never!" he argued.

Suddenly there was a scream like an angry elephant. Krawlie was coming to get him! "You-don't-get-away-that-easy-darling-Dason," she cried.

"You wouldn't do this to me, Betty!" Danny screeched as Krawlie reached out her octopus arms towards him.

"So let me be the captain of Space Eagle!" I said.

"No! No! No! Never!" he gasped.

Just then the feather on the end of Krawlie-Me-Lug's tentacle touched his neck and one of her ten-kilo clogs crushed his toe.

"Aieee! Yes! Yes! Yes! I agree!" he howled.

I opened the door. He jumped in and I slammed it shut after him. He lay panting on the cabin floor while I started the Space Eagle and set course for Earth.

"You know, Danny," I said as I gave him a cup of tea, "I think you really should retire!"

"You know," he moaned, "I think you're right! I'll get my garden finished. I've always wanted a fish pond."

"You can grow flowers in your garden!"

He nodded happily. "Roses!"

"Pansies," I said.

"Tulips!" he said.

"Wallflowers," I said.

"Daffodils," he said.

"And Geraniums?" I asked.

Dan Darenot grinned. He shook his head slowly. "No," he said. "No geraniums… I never want to see a Geranium as long as I live!"

I think I know what he means.

This is Captain Betty Yett signing off.

The world next door

Old Mrs Quill lived in a little black and white house by the side of a wood. Next to the house was an orchard, with twelve apple trees. In the spring the trees were covered with pink and white flowers. In the autumn they were hung all over with red and yellow fruit. Mrs Quill sold some of the apples, and gave many away to her friends, and ate the rest. And, as well, she made money by washing people's shirts and sheets and towels. She had clothes-lines hung between the apple trees, and every windy day there would be white and coloured laundry like flags blowing among the branches. The wind always blew on Mrs Quill's washdays.

"The wind is my friend," said Mrs Quill.

Besides washing, Mrs Quill knew a great deal about how to cure pain. She often went into the wood, where she picked leaves and flowers and berries. From these she made pastes and pills and drinks which would send away almost any pain, headache, sore throat, stomach ache or stiffness in the legs.

Mrs Quill gave her medicines to people; she never wanted money for her treatment.

"Everything in the wood is free," she said.

"How do you know so much, Mrs Quill?" a boy called Pip asked her.

"The wind tells me," she said. "I listen to the wind, in the leaves, in the branches. The wind comes from another world. My cottage stands by the wood. And the wood grows by a mountain. In the same way, this world floats by another world. And that is where the wind comes from."

Mrs Quill's old cat, Foss, purred and rubbed against her ankles.

"Foss knows about the wind," she said. "Foss goes into the wood at night, and hears it whispering secrets."

One day, a big car stopped outside Mrs Quill's cottage, and a white-haired man got out. His name was Sir Groby Griddle.

"I am your new landlord, Mrs Quill," he said. "I have bought the wood, and the orchard, and the mountain. I plan to knock down your house and put a golf course on this land. You must find somewhere else to live."

"Leave my house?" said Mrs Quill. "But I was born in this house. I have always lived here. And so did my mother and grandmother."

"I can't help that," said Sir Groby. "The house has to come down. You will be found another one, somewhere else. Anywhere you like."

"But there would be no apple trees. And no wood where I could find plants. And nowhere to hang the washing."

They were standing under the apple trees as they talked. A white sheet blew out and flapped itself round Sir Groby. This annoyed him.

"All those apple trees must be cut down," he said. "They are old and crooked. And the wood must come down as well. There will be a main road leading to the golf course. And a car park. And a club house and a tea room."

Mrs Quill said, "My cottage is very old. Hundreds and hundreds of years old. There is a law which says that old houses must not be pulled down."

The wind blew again, and a pillow case flapped across Sir Groby's face. He was even more annoyed, because what Mrs Quill said was true.

"You have not heard the last of this," he said.

He stamped away. A long roller towel blew out and wrapped round his neck. He shouted, "You'll see, very soon! I always get my way in the end!"

After that, for many weeks, Mrs Quill was very quiet, thinking. She did not often smile. When people came to her house, asking for headache pills, or syrup for a sore throat, she was not always there.

"Where have you been, Mrs Quill?" the boy called Pip asked her one day, as she bandaged his grazed knee.

"In the wood. Tying threads round the trees."

"All the trees, Mrs Quill?"

"Yes, every one."

"Why?"

"So that they will know me again. And I shall know them."

Now autumn had come. Mrs Quill's apples had all been picked. Lots of people helped her. The apples had been laid on shelves in her shed. They had a cool, sharp smell, which came floating out of the doorway, on the wind.

Once a year, Mrs Quill used to catch a bus and go into town to buy needles, and soap, and a new saucepan, and a garden fork. Things like that.

This year, on her way home, as she stood waiting by the bus stop, she noticed a little black and white house on a patch of waste land nearby.

"That looks like my house," thought Mrs Quill.

But then a woman asked what would be good for her

little boy's ear-ache, and a man wanted a cure for chilblains. And then the bus arrived and Mrs Quill got on it, with her bundles.

But when she came to where her house had been, it was gone. The shed had been pulled down too. Apples were lying all over the ground, some of them squashed. And there stood Sir Groby, smiling all over his face. Men were in the orchard, sawing down the apple trees.

"I have had your house moved," Sir Groby told Mrs Quill. "I had it put on a truck, and moved to the edge of the town. That's quite legal. That's where you'll find it. It will be better for you there. You can go shopping, and see more people."

"Where is my cat, Foss?" said Mrs Quill.

"He ran off into the wood," said a man who was half-way through sawing down a tree. "We'll find him tomorrow. We are going to cut down the whole wood."

Mrs Quill stood still for a moment.

"Then I had better go into the wood now," she said to Sir Groby. And she added, "You are going to miss that wood. You are going to need it. And the orchard, my orchard, that your men have cut down. You will be thirsty. All you can think about will be an apple. Your head will ache in the hot sun. All you need will be shade. But there will be no apple for you, and no shade."

A dry gust of wind blew from the wood and flung a handful of leaves against Sir Groby. They stung his eyes and scratched his cheeks. He shook his head angrily. When he could see again, Mrs Quill was walking away from him, into the wood.

"Let her go, silly old fool!" he said. "She'll come out soon enough, when we start cutting down the trees."

But Mrs Quill did not come out of the wood.

And when, next day, Sir Groby's men began cutting down the trees, a queer thing happened.

As each tree was cut down, it shrank, like a slip of paper when you set a match to it, and vanished clean away. At the end of the day, instead of a huge pile of tree trunks, ready to be sold for timber, there was just nothing at all. Only some mud and a few leaves.

The roots were dug up and the land made flat and level. A golf course was laid out, and a car park. A red brick club house was built, with a flag on it.

But very few people came to play golf on the golf course. The ones who did, told their friends that, at night, after playing, they had bad dreams. They dreamed they were trying to play golf in a forest. Trees and bushes grew up all round them. Leaves and prickles grew out of their golf clubs. Their balls rolled down rabbit holes.

Nobody came back to play on Sir Groby's course a second time. He made no money from it.

The club house stood empty. The flag dangled from its pole. No wind ever blew.

Sir Groby himself fell ill. His head ached all the time. Nothing would help the ache. All day long he was thirsty. He drank water, beer, milk, soda, wine, tea, coffee and champagne, but no drink would make the thirst go away.

And, every night, he dreamed about walking in a dark wood and listening to the wind.

At last he was so ill that he had to be taken to hospital.

"Where is Mrs Quill?" he kept asking. "And why does the wind never blow any more?"

"The wind *is* blowing, Sir Groby," the nurses told him. "A gale is blowing, outside the window, at this very minute. Can't you hear it?"

But he could hear nothing.

He lay ill for weeks and weeks. Nobody cared about him, so nobody came to see him, except a boy called Pip.

"I dream about Mrs Quill every night," Pip told Sir Groby. "In my dream I see her living in her cottage, with her wood, and her orchard. She is living in the world that floats next door to this one. You won't see her again."

"I don't want to hear about your dreams! All I want is something to cure this awful thirst," croaked Sir Groby.

"When I next see Mrs Quill in my dream I will ask her," said Pip.

Next day Pip came to the hospital again.

"In my dream, I asked Mrs Quill about your thirst," he told Sir Groby. "She says that only an apple from her orchard will cure it."

"I don't believe you!" growled Sir Groby. "That's rubbish! In any case, her orchard is cut down, and there are no apples left."

A sudden gust of wind blew through the hospital room where Sir Groby lay. The window curtain sailed inwards and wrapped itself round Sir Groby's angry face. And a shower of dead leaves swept through the window like arrows and landed all over Sir Groby's bed.

"Good gracious!" cried a nurse, coming in. And she ran for a dustpan.

Sir Groby lay scowling, and said nothing at all for the rest of the day. That night he dreamed that he was standing on the edge of the world, looking across the gap at the world that lay next door.

There was Mrs Quill's black and white cottage, beside the orchard, beside the wood, beside the mountain. There was Mrs Quill herself, hanging out her washing, sheets and towels and pillow cases, among the old twisted apple trees.

"I'm thirsty!" called Sir Groby, across the gap. "Oh, Mrs Quill, won't you help me? I'm so terribly thirsty!"

But Mrs Quill took no notice, just went on pegging out the towels and teacloths.

"Mrs Quill! I'm sorry I moved your house! I'm sorry I cut down your orchard! I'm sorry I cut down your wood! Won't you please tell me what will stop this awful thirst?"

At that Mrs Quill turned and looked at him.

"Just being sorry is not enough," she said. "Hundreds of creatures had their homes in that wood – birds and mice, foxes, squirrels, rabbits, spiders, adders, bats, otters, hares and weasels. How can you put right the harm you did?"

"But I'm so thirsty!"

"Only an apple from my orchard will cure your thirst."

"But there aren't any left! They were all squashed and trampled."

"I have just two left here," she said. "See if you can catch one."

And she threw an apple across the gap.

But Sir Groby was not able to catch it. Down it fell – down and down – into the gap between the worlds, and was lost.

Mrs Quill turned and walked away into her orchard.

And Sir Groby, crying and wailing like a two-year-old, woke up from his dream.

Next day he told the people at the hospital that he wanted to leave and go home.

"But you are not better," they said.

"I shall never be better if I stay here," said Sir Groby.

He sent for a car and a driver to come and fetch him.

On the way to Sir Groby's home, his car passed the bus stop where Mrs Quill had caught her bus. But there was no black and white cottage on the site where Sir Groby's men had left it. Just a bare patch of ground with some bits of paper blowing about.

The boy, Pip, was standing and looking at the empty space.

Sir Groby opened his car window and called, "What happened to Mrs Quill's house?"

"It has gone," said Pip. "Just like the trees."

Sir Groby went home to his large, grand house. He ate roast beef for his supper, and drank champagne. But his head just ached, just as badly as ever, and he was still thirsty.

At night, as he lay in bed, he heard the voices of all the creatures he had turned out of their homes, crying and grieving, squeaking and squawking, chirping and cheeping and chirruping.

He dreamed that he saw Mrs Quill, busy in the world next door, hanging out her washing. The wind was helping her.

"Mrs Quill! I will plant another wood, I promise!" he called to her across the gap. "Only, please, please, throw me one of your apples! I will plant another wood, and an orchard beside it."

At that she turned and looked at him more kindly.

"I have one more apple," she said. "See if you can catch it this time."

She tossed an apple across the gap. This time the wind gusted and blew the apple so that Sir Groby was just able to grab it.

But as he was about to take a big bite of it, he woke up.

Oh, what a blow that was, to wake and find he had no apple in his hand!

Sir Groby wailed like a two-year-old.

But then he struggled out of bed, and dragged on his clothes, and picked up his telephone, and gave orders for the golf club house to be pulled down, and the car park dug up, and the golf course ploughed all over.

He ordered his car, and told the driver to take him to the golf course. On the way they passed by the bus stop, where Mrs Quill's house had been left. Sir Groby noticed that the empty waste patch was all covered with small green shoots, with young new leaves on them.

For it was spring by now.

Sir Groby told his driver to stop, and got out of the car.

The boy Pip was standing and looking at the small trees.

"They are all seedling apple trees," he said.

A warm spring wind was blowing. It tossed the sprigs and leaves of the little seedling trees. The wind had a cool, sharp smell.

As it blew against his face, Sir Groby felt that the wind had come from a very long way off. Perhaps from another world. Perhaps from the world next door.

The bus stop that ate children

Precious thought the bus stop was a witch. She had nightmares about it. But it's not what you're thinking – she wasn't crazy. You, too, might have had nightmares about that particular bus stop.

But on that Saturday morning, being scared of the bus stop was very inconvenient. For Precious had to wait by it, for the bus to town. She was going to market. Her mother was busy, having the new baby. Kapito, her big brother, was chopping maize out in the fields. So it was up to Precious to do the shopping.

She didn't mind that. She was proud of being given the responsibility. But she wished, with all her heart, that the bus would turn up soon.

"Rice, cassava, beans," said Precious to herself. Those were the things she had to buy at the market.

Precious tried to keep a safe distance from the bus stop. She looked up and down the road. Empty. Except for a goat. No one came to wait with her, to protect her if the bus stop should turn nasty.

She had to wait alone.

The bus stop was a baobab tree – a massive tree with a swollen lumpy trunk. It was hollow inside. It made a great bus stop. Six or seven people could shelter inside it from the sun. But nothing would make Precious shelter inside the trunk of that old baobab tree.

When she was very small, Kapito had said: "That tree is a witch tree. Look at her warty face, her long bony fingers."

And it was true that, if you stared very hard at the trunk you could see a face there. It was a scowling face, with a big hooky nose. And the thin, whippy twigs did look like fingers – or claws. The baobab was a thousand years old. It was the kind of tree you could believe all sorts of things about.

But Precious was ten years old now. She had responsibilities. And she tried not to believe the stories that Kapito told her. This was harder than it might seem, for Kapito was a brilliant story teller. He loved telling scary stories. He liked to frighten you if he could. It made him feel good.

Kapito had told her, for instance, that there were spirits living in the thatch of their hut. They slid out at night to guzzle on the blood of sleeping children and grow fat.

He had told her that the walking dead prowled round their hut at night. They called, "Whoo, whoo!" for you to come and join them in their cold and lonely graves.

Precious didn't believe any of that stuff any more. But, stupidly, she couldn't help feeling that the bus stop was a witch.

"What's wrong with you, Precious?" she scolded herself, as she waited for the bus to town. "You're grown up now. And scared out of your wits by bus stops? Shame on you!"

She held her grass basket over her head like an umbrella to shade her from the sun. She looked up and down the road in both directions. Empty.

Precious shivered. She couldn't help recalling Kapito's story about the witch tree.

"That place where you wait," Kapito had said, "where you wait for the bus inside the tree – that is the witch's belly. It's okay when grown-ups wait there. But when children wait for the bus, all on their own, the witch's belly begins to rumble. That means she is hungry. And then, zip, just like zipping up your clothes, the witch tree closes up with the child inside it. The child may shout and scream. No one will hear. And after some time, the witch tree opens up again. But where is the child? The child is nowhere to be seen. The bus stop is empty."

And Precious had said: "Where is the child?" even though she already knew the answer.

"The witch tree has eaten her, of course," Kapito had answered. "Even her bones. But the witch does not eat them all. If her belly is full she keeps the child, until she is hungry. Do you see those bumps on the trunk of the witch tree?"

Precious saw them.

"That is the witch's larder," said Kapito. "Put your ear close. You will hear the child inside, calling out for help."

"Don't be silly," Precious said. "You're only trying to frighten me. There is no child in there."

She put her ear against the witch tree's largest bump to show she was not scared. But then she leapt back in horror. She had heard the child! A tiny piping voice inside the trunk!

"See! I told you," Kapito said. "You remember that small child who went missing from the next village?"

"But everybody says a leopard took him, or a hyena."

"They don't know anything," Kapito said. "That child was probably waiting at this bus stop, on his own. That poor child is probably inside that lump on the witch tree. It is his voice you are hearing now. What did he say?"

"I don't know," said Precious, miserably.

"I bet he said, 'Help me, Help me,' " said Kapito. "But nobody can help him. The witch tree has got him."

So that is why Precious, on that Saturday morning, was keeping a safe distance from the bus stop.

But then she heard something. It made her blood turn icy cold, even in that fierce sun.

Tap, tap, tap, tap.

It was the largest bump on the witch tree. The one where Kapito said the poor lost child was trapped. He was trying to escape!

Tap, tap. A hole appeared in the trunk.

"Aiee!" cried Precious, terrified. If she hadn't had a bus to catch, she would've run away.

The hole got larger. Soon a finger would poke through, or a hand! Then the head of the poor lost child would follow!

But none of these things happened.

Squeezing through the hole in the witch tree came a tiny, rumpled baby bird. It flopped onto the nearest branch, exhausted.

Precious forgot how scared she was. She forgot that the witch tree might zip her up inside and eat her. She came up close. She put her eye against the hole.

"Kapito," she grinned to herself. "You are the world's greatest liar."

For inside the witch tree was not a poor lost child but a nest of hornbill chicks. The mother bird had sealed them in with mud to keep them safe – safe from snakes and eagles. But now they had hatched. And they were breaking out, one by one.

The mother bird was on the topmost branch of the witch tree. She was calling her chicks to join her.

Tap, tap, tap, tap. Another chick came tumbling out. Precious laughed.

"I never really thought," she told herself, "that the bus stop would eat me. Only someone with a head as empty as this basket would think that!"

"You want this bus or not?" called the bus driver. The bus had come, without Precious even noticing.

Precious sat on the bus. "Cassava, beans, rice," she said, so she didn't forget.

Then she thought about the new baby. Maybe it

would have arrived by the time that she got home.

Would Precious tell her new brother or sister scary stories about the child-eating bus stop? Stories like the ones Kapito told her?

Of course she would.

For it would be a great shame, wouldn't it, to waste a good story!

The greatest drummer in the world

I hope they shrivel up like burnt matchsticks. I hope
spiders crawl all over their dreams. I hope giants come
and turn their bones to jelly. They've banned me. They
won't let me play my drums. Too loud, they say. They
can't stand the noise. Noise! That's not noise, I tell
them. That's music. That's rhythm. That's me making
my drums talk. You've got to let me play. Enough, they
say. It's driving them mad. It's making their ears buzz,
their heads pound and their nerves jangle. No more
drumming.

Can you believe that? Just when I'm starting to be
really good. If I practise, I could be the greatest
drummer in the world. I tell them that. I tell them I've
got to practise. I'm going to be the greatest drummer in
the world. They just laugh. No more drumming, they
say. Not here. Not there. Not anywhere we can hear
you.

They don't understand. There's magic in my drum.
There are stories that will amaze the world, if I'm
allowed to tell them. When I play my drum, the cats

arch their backs and the dogs howl at the moon. The crickets are silent in the long grass and the ripe mangoes drop from the branches. It's true. The trees and the flowers dance to the rhythm of my drumming.

When I'm playing the drum, there's nothing I can't do.

The other day, I was beating up a storm – *crash, thrum, rat-a-tat-tat, boom boom* – you should have heard it. All the kids of the village were laughing and kicking up their heels and leaping and dancing and flinging their bodies this way and that. Then the grown-ups charged in and ordered us to stop. They said we were making too much noise. They said the whole village was shaking. The walls were cracking. They couldn't work. They couldn't even hear themselves think. No more drumming, they said. Not here, not there, not any place they could hear me.

So what can I do? Where can I go? If I play again, they say they'll burn my drum. But if I don't play, I'll explode. There'll be nothing left of me. So I have to leave. I have to take my drum and leave this village and go into the forest, into the deepest part of the forest where no-one will be able to hear my drum. That's what I must do…

Strange things have been happening. I've lived in the forest now for a month. I've built myself a tree hut. I live on blackberries and nettle soup and wild mushrooms and fish from the stream which I cook over a wood fire. And I play my drum. I play all day and all night sometimes, for as long as I like and no-one is here to stop me. I play to the birds and the wind in the trees and the empty sky. In the morning, I drum the sun awake. At night, the stars gather in the sky to listen to the magic of my drumming.

But I miss my friends. I hoped some of them would come with me. I thought Mackie, at least, would come with me. He's my best friend. But he didn't come. None of them did. Yes, they said, they would have come with me if they could but their life was in the village and, well, you know how it is. So they just wished me good luck and hoped I would become the greatest drummer in the world.

I miss them. But Mackie comes to see me every day. He brings me bread and milk and cheese and the latest news from the village. I think the elders of the village are sending him to keep an eye on me. I suppose they'd feel bad if anything happened to me. But I can look after myself. By all accounts, it's they who need looking after. Because strange things have been happening, as I told you. It's like a curse, Mackie says. A curse has been put on the village. On the night that I left, there was a great storm. Lightning struck the main house where the elders meet and burnt it to the ground. And this is strange because in the forest, which is not so far from the village, there was no storm. I slept my first night

under a great umbrella tree and it was calm and peaceful. No hailstones fell from the sky. I heard no thunder, saw no lightning. Perhaps my drum in its rage conjured up the storm and hurled it against the village.

Mackie said that a few days after I left, some of the cattle started to sicken. They wouldn't eat. They grew thinner and thinner. Nobody could discover what was wrong with them. In the end, they turned black and shrivelled up and died. It was a great blow to the village.

After that it was the spiders. Hundreds of them. As big as your fist. As big as crabs. That's what Mackie said. Scuttling about everywhere. They had to ask the spider monkey in to get rid of them. I hate spiders. I'm scared of them. I'm glad I wasn't in the village when the spiders came.

And now the worst thing of all. Mackie brought me the news last week. A giant. A real giant, taller than the tallest tree with a voice like thunder. He's been terrorizing the village. He's been making them feed him with everything they've got. He's been eating cows and goats and vegetables and fruit from the trees. Everything. Soon there'll be nothing left and they're afraid he'll start eating the people. They think the children will be first. They don't know what to do.

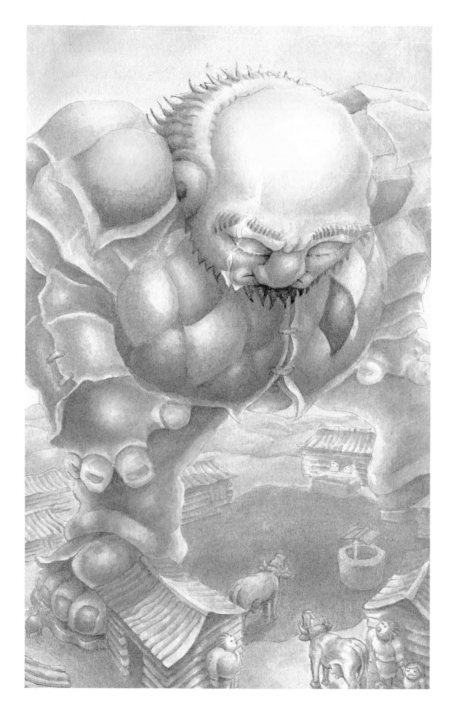

Every day he comes and demands food in a voice like thunder. They feel small and helpless. What can they do? They can't fight him. He's too big and strong. He could crush them with one stamp of his foot.

I feel bad. I feel miserable. I feel it's my fault. According to Mackie, some of the villagers are blaming me, too. I know in my wicked temper I cursed the village. I wished bad things on them. But I didn't mean it, not really. It's my village, after all, and we are all one family. I don't wish them any harm. I only want to be allowed to play my drum. But now I'm frightened. If anything happens to the village, to the people in the village, I'll be lost. I'll be completely alone. I have to do something. I have to save them to save myself. But how?

Mackie came again an hour ago. The villagers are desperate. They are thinking of abandoning the village and going somewhere else to escape from the giant. If he comes back tomorrow, they say, they will take what they can carry with them and flee.

"What about me?" I said. "What shall I do? I'll be left alone in this forest for ever."

"Come with us," Mackie said. "Come back to us."

"And my drum?"

"There are more important things than drumming."

I thought for a moment. Then I made my decision. I didn't know if it would work out but I had to try it.

"Tell them not to go," I said. "Tell them I will save them from the giant."

"You? How?"

"Just tell them that," I said. "Tell them that if I can bring my drum, if they will let me play my drum, I will save them from the giant."

"They won't believe you," Mackie said. "They don't believe children can do anything."

"What choice do they have?" I said. "There is nothing they can do."

Mackie has been gone for an hour now. I am waiting for him to come back with an answer.

Mackie was so out of breath, he could hardly talk. He'd been running all the way.

"Yes," he panted. "They agree. Whatever you want if you can save them from the giant."

They don't really believe I can help them, I know. They're so desperate and I'm their last hope. But I know they don't really believe in me. Still I will try and save them. I'll try my best. But first I must spend a little time by myself. I must thank the spirits of the forest and the earth and the stream for feeding me, for looking after me. Then I must prepare myself.

"Go back," I call to Mackie. "I will come soon."

They tell me the giant always comes over the hill to the village. He takes such enormous strides that in no time at all he's there at the village. He waits outside the walls while the villagers bring him cows, barrels of goats' milk, waggon loads of vegetables, whatever they can find. They can hardly believe how much he eats. For him, a whole loaf of bread is just a small bite.

So I've set myself up with my drum in a field outside the village from where I can see the hill. And I wait. No-one ever knows when the giant is going to come. Sometimes it's the mornings, sometimes it's the afternoons. Sometimes he doesn't come until late at night. No-one ever knows. So I wait. I sit cross-legged on the long grass, my drum between my knees, the sticks ready in my hands. And I wait. I stare at the white hill over which the giant will come. Behind the hill, the sky is a dark blue colour, like a bruise. The sun is a dull red. The wind rustles the grass. I can hear the *chirr-chirr-chirring* of the crickets. The air is so heavy I can hardly breathe. Everyone is anxious, waiting in silence.

The hours pass. The sun is slowly sinking. Perhaps, I think to myself, the giant won't come today. Perhaps he won't come at all. Perhaps he's gone away. I feel disappointed at the thought and immediately afterwards I'm full of guilt. I must not be so selfish. But I want him to come now. I want to test my drum against his greatness.

What's this? The ground is trembling. It feels like an earthquake. A spiral of dust spins over the hill. A whisper rises on the wind: "It's the giant. He's coming."

And there he is, standing on top of the hill. I see a massive dark shape silhouetted against the fading light of the sky. My hands are shaking. My bones are turning to jelly. If I could, I would run but I cannot move. He is striding nearer. He is in the field. Let him not tread on me. Let him not trample on me with his great feet.

He stops. I look up at him. I can sense him thinking to himself: "What is this insignificant little insect?" He has a long mournful face, the face of someone who has never laughed. And in that instant, I lose my fear. My hands stop shaking. I am calm and clear-headed. He is a man, after all. A big, strong man, certainly, but still – a man. He's not a god or a magic spirit.

Lightly at first, the sticks begin to beat out a rhythm on the drum. The giant looks puzzled. The drum rhythm grows louder, more insistent. *Boom-boom rat-a-tat-tat vroom-vroom rat-a-tat-tat.* The sound rolls over the fields and the hills and echoes up to the sky. I am swinging into the rhythm now. I am losing myself in the rhythmic drumbeats. I am making the drum talk. We are as one, me and the drum. My drum is telling a story that will amaze the world.

The giant shifts from side to side uneasily. His feet are itching, his knees are twitching. He can't understand what is happening. He hops from one foot to the other. He begins to move to the rhythm of the drum. He is dancing. With jerky giant steps he is dancing round and round. Give him plenty of space. Mind he doesn't tread on anyone. He can't help himself. He is at the mercy of his feet. He is at the mercy of my drum.

"Stop!" orders the giant in his booming voice. "Stop!"

But I don't stop. I am conjuring up a magic giant dance. My drumbeats are forcing the giant to move to their rhythm. On and on and round and round he dances, spinning, twirling, raising his knees high, clomping down with his great feet. What a sight! What a noise! The earth is vibrating to the throb of my drum and the pounding feet of the giant.

The moon comes up and the stars peep out and still I play and still he dances, while the villagers watch and hold their breath. What will be the end of my drum story?

By the morning, the giant, prancing dizzily, is in a state of panic, pleading with me to stop, begging for mercy. But I am relentless. My arms and wrists are aching but I can't stop now. Not now when I'm coming up to the grand finale, the climax of the story.

Gradually, I drop the cross rhythms. I let the dance beats simplify into the heavy *one-two* rhythm of a march. The giant stops twirling round. He looks like an enormous mechanical toy that is winding down. And then to the urgent *pom-pom* beat of my drum, he marches off, away from the village, on and up and over the hill and on and on he marches. And for all I know, he is marching still. Certainly, the village has neither seen him nor heard anything of him since.

Only then do I stop playing. Suddenly, tears stream down my cheeks. Perhaps it's exhaustion, perhaps it's relief, I don't know. But I'm hugging my drum and weeping buckets. I can hear applause from the villagers, cheers from the children, but still I weep.

One of the elders who is my uncle comes to me and raises me to my feet. Then he bows and says: "We thank you. You may be only a slip of a child but you are indeed the greatest drummer in the world."

I look at him. Inside, I am smiling. "Can I play my drum then?" I ask him.

"A promise is a promise," he says. "We were wrong to forbid you to play your drum. And now that you have saved us from the giant, we owe you a great debt. But I would ask you to consider this. If you play your drum anywhere you please at any time of the day or night, you will be disturbing the peace of the village. You will be upsetting people and making them angry. Do you want to do that?"

I shake my head.

"Do you think we can come to some arrangement?"

I nod. I don't want to have to go and live by myself in the forest again.

"Well then," he continues, "consider this. We will build you a special drum house. We will make it so that the sound stays inside the house as far as is possible. You will be able to play there whenever you like in the hours of daylight but not in the hours of darkness. And once a week on a Sunday, you will play for us in the village square and we will all dance the story of how your drum defeated the giant. What do you think?"

I can't speak. I go to him and embrace him. I am happier than he can ever know.

And that's how it was and that's how it is. My story soon spread around the countryside. If you come to my part of the world, you are sure to hear it for everyone is talking about me, the drummer girl who saved her village from the terrible giant.

Perhaps I really am the greatest drummer in the world.